Children love this book!

The full-color version of *My Friend with Autism* is designed for peers of children with autism. This book explains what autism is in a positive and understandable way, and how the behavior of children with autism can be different from that of neurotypical children. Helping neurotypical children understand their classmates will encourage positive relationships and help to grow meaningful friendships among peers.

Teachers love this book!

Teachers will find this book invaluable in helping to integrate students with autism spectrum disorders into the neurotypical student group.

Printable coloring pages to reinforce the lessons of the book can be found at this link: https://www.fhautism.com/mfwa-coloring-pages/

These printed pages can be taken home and shared with parents. As students share the pages of this book with their parents, it will reinforce the child's learning and reassure parents that students with autism are indeed extraordinary, and that they present an exceptional opportunity for learning and interaction.

Anyone who knows a child with autism love this book!

The "Getting to Know a Child with Autism" section at the back is useful for babysitters, friends, church members, neighbors, and anyone who comes into contact with a child with autism. This useful, thought-provoking section provides further information relating to each page in the children's section.

Every young mind—whether we call it neurotypical or autistic—is different. Each is good at some things, and each has difficulty with other things. What is most important is remembering that each mind—each child—is valuable. All children have the potential to contribute great and important things to the world.

My Friend with Autism

All marketing and publishing rights guaranteed to and reserved by:

FUTURE HORIZONS INC.

800-489-0727, 817-277-0727, 817-277-2270 Fax

Website: www.FHautism.com, E-mail: info@FHautism.com

Digital color enhancement of illustrations by Matt Mitchell

Publisher's Cataloging-In-Publication Data
(Prepared by The Donohue Group, Inc.)

Bishop, Beverly.

  My friend with autism / written by Beverly Bishop ; illustrated by Craig Bishop.

  Interest age group: 006-012.

  ISBN: 9781949177503

  1. Autism--Juvenile fiction. 2. Friendship in children--Juvenile fiction. 3. Autistic children--Juvenile fiction. 4. Children with mental disabilities--Social networks--Juvenile fiction. 5. Autism--Fiction. 6. Friendship--Fiction. 7. Autistic children--Fiction. I. Bishop, Craig. II. Title.

PZ7.B5243 My 2020
[Fic]

This book is dedicated to Seth's Grandmas.
Their influence on Seth and our entire family
will long surpass the number of earthly years
they were able to spend with us.

Foreword

For as long as I can remember, people of all ages and backgrounds have approached my mother after writing this book. Teachers and classmates have explained how they now view their students with autism and their peers in a different light. Parents and grandparents have thanked her for raising awareness on how their children with autism communicate. Siblings have expressed gratitude for its attempt at normalizing interactions.

For many people with autism over the past 18 years, this book has taught others how our minds operate, how we perceive the world, and how we form connections with people. It expresses our achievements and our shortcomings in a way that I could never adequately express. It is safe to say that this book has directly led to more people understanding my odd behaviors and, to be frank, is probably the only reason why I had friends in elementary school.

However, this book can only say so much about how our minds tick. Our individuality makes this subject quite complex, and you can only fit so many pages into a children's book. Breakthroughs in our understanding of autism will keep occurring, and we can only update this book so many times. Depending on how long it has been and who you are interacting with, just reading this book can only get you so far.

Because of this, do not just think of this book as a hub of knowledge on how to interact with people with autism. Rather, think of it as a set of tools which you can use to chip away at our brains and see for yourself how we tick. Through that chipping away, you will not only come to understand how we perceive the world, but also have an opportunity to affect our own.

To quote American author Dan Brown, "Knowledge is a tool, and like all tools, its impact is in the hands of the user."

You have your tools. What impact you leave behind is now in your hands.

— Sebastian "Seth" Bishop

I have a friend with autism. He is good at many things.

My friend's ears work really well. He can hear sounds I may not even hear. He is almost always the first one to hear an airplane or a train coming. This is why he sometimes covers his ears even when things don't seem loud to me.

My friend's eyes work really well. He sees little things that I might not even notice. His eyes work so well that bright lights or a sunny day will often hurt his eyes.

My friend's sense of taste works really well. He can taste even a little bit of pepper in his food. This is why he only eats certain foods, and why he sometimes doesn't want foods that are too hot or cold.

My friend has a strong sense of touch. He can feel even the smallest little thing touching him. This makes him very ticklish. Sometimes he doesn't like to be touched. Other times, his sense of touch makes him want to touch me. If I don't want him to touch me, I ask him nicely not to touch me.

My friend is very strong. Sometimes he forgets how strong he is, and he gives hugs that are too hard. Sometimes he plays too roughly with me. I can help him by reminding him to be gentle and by remembering not to play too roughly myself.

I can help my friend by playing games with lots of moving, running, dancing, or swinging. When I play with my friend, I do not have to worry that I will get autism, because autism cannot be caught like a cold or the flu.

My friend is very smart. He is good at counting, the alphabet, and many other things. He knew the letters of the alphabet even when he was a little boy. My friend likes when we play with letters and numbers, like when we spell or count.

Just like me, my friend is good at playing. He especially loves to play with cars, trucks, trains, and things that spin. Sometimes he plays differently than I do, so I watch the way he plays and then I try to do what he is doing, right next to him. Sometimes he will watch me play and then he might try doing what I like to do.

My friend with autism is good at many things,
but his autism also makes some things hard for him.

Talking is sometimes hard for my friend. But when he doesn't talk, my feelings are not hurt because I understand that talking is hard for him. Sometimes I can even help him by suggesting some words he might want to say.

My friend may still want to play with me even if he doesn't talk much. I just keep playing and talking with him, even if he doesn't talk or if his words don't make sense to me.

Understanding other people's feelings is hard for my friend.
He does not always understand that I have feelings, too. When I see
a person crying, I know that the person is probably sad. But when my
friend sees a person crying, he may not understand what it means.

Sharing is hard for my friend. He doesn't understand how much fun it can be to share his toys, or that my feelings are hurt when he takes toys away from me. Sometimes I ask my friend to share with me, but he says no or he does not answer me. If I think he really should be sharing, I usually ask an adult for help.

Change is often very hard for my friend. When he is doing one thing and it is time to start doing something different, he gets frustrated. I try to help by telling him what is going to happen next. For example, just before recess, I remind him that we'll be going outside in just a few minutes.

Sitting still and quiet is hard for my friend. When it is time to sit quietly, I can help him by showing him how well I sit quietly. Sometimes I can also help by reminding him to use a quiet voice.

Because some things are hard for my friend, adults may use pictures to help him understand better. I like seeing his pictures and learning what they mean. Sometimes I can use his pictures to help him with things like sharing, changing activities, or understanding feelings.

17

Just like me, my friend does many things very well,
and some things are hard for him.

And just like me, my friend with autism loves to have friends!

Getting to Know a Child with Autism

The purpose of this section is to provide adults with additional information about autism based on themes from each page in the children's portion of this book, as well as ideas for helping a child with autism. This is not an exhaustive or scientific discussion of autism. Instead, it is intended to be a quick read and a helpful tool to be shared with friends, family, teachers, parents, or others. The goal is to give enough understanding to encourage meaningful relationships and help reduce any fears that people who are new to autism may have. This information is intended for adults, not children, so please use your best judgment and choose talking points that are appropriate for your audience.

Autism is four times more prevalent in males than females. Therefore, in order to avoid the clumsiness of him/her, masculine pronouns are used. It is not in any way intended to exclude girls who are affected by autism.

Page-by-Page Notes for Adults

Page 1 - What is autism?

- **Autism is classified as a spectrum disorder (ASD)** because the degree to which a person is affected can vary greatly. The traits of two people with autism may be completely different. The spectrum ranges from children who are considered aloof (usually unable to speak and seemingly separated from the world) to "high-functioning" (speaking fluently and able to interact with peers). The behaviors described in this book are typical of children with "high-functioning autism" (formerly referred to as Asperger's syndrome).

- **Each child with autism is unique.** Some of the traits in this book may describe a particular child with autism exactly, while other traits don't match that same child at all. These variations make every child with autism one-of-a-kind, just like every other child.

- **As of 2016, the CDC estimates that about 1 in 59 children has been identified with ASD** (16.8 per 1,000 8-year-olds). Two other independent studies published in *Pediatrics* and *JAMA Pediatrics* estimate that 1 in 40 children has ASD.

- **Presently, there is no single known cause of autism.** Genetic and environmental components, along with other factors, probably cause many different types of autism. Researchers have identified a number of genes associated with ASD. Children are likely born with a susceptibility to autism, but researchers have not identified the exact "triggers" that may cause autism to develop within the first three years of life.

- **Autism affects the way the brain interprets and communicates information.** Imaging studies confirm developmental differences in several regions of the brains of people with autism. These differences may be the result of disruptions in normal brain growth during early development, affecting how brain cells communicate with one another.

- **A person cannot outgrow autism;** however, many strategies and treatments—especially in the early years—have proven very successful in decreasing challenges.

- **Sensory sensitivities are often inconsistent.** Each sense can be either over-sensitive or under-sensitive, and the level of sensitivity may actually change daily or throughout the day. Think of it this way: the connections between the senses and the brain seem to have short circuits—sometimes they work too well, and sometimes they don't work at all.

Page 2 – Hearing

- **Many adults with autism have described their hearing as having no background noise,** as if everything they hear comes in at the same volume or level of importance. Imagine simultaneously hearing someone talking to you, the refrigerator fan, other people in the room having conversations, and an airplane flying overhead, all at the same volume. It would be difficult to distinguish important sounds from unimportant ones. What would seem a "normal" or even unnoticeable background noise to a neurotypical person might be overwhelming to a person with autism.

- **Some sounds may actually cause physical pain.**

- **Unpredictable or sudden sounds may be scary to a child with autism.** Even if he can anticipate the noise, not knowing its exact timing can cause anxiety (when will the dryer buzz?).

- **Help the child focus on what is important.** Make sure that the child is paying attention before speaking and talk directly to him. A sudden temper tantrum or other undesired behavior can be caused by too much noise, or by a particular noise that disturbs the child. It sometimes takes detective work to discover exactly what is upsetting a child.

- **Children with autism are trying to communicate through behavior**. Try to figure out what the child is attempting to communicate and respond appropriately. When in loud or busy environments, it may be useful to allow breaks in quiet places. Warning the child before an upcoming sound (fire drills, whistles, vacuum cleaners, drills, mixers, etc.) may also be helpful if the timing can be predicted exactly. Sometimes, however, waiting for an unpredictable sound and the resulting pain causes much more anxiety than the unexpected sound would have.

Page 3 – Vision

- **A child may see things others cannot see, such as light patterns, the individual dots of color that make up a picture, or the words printed on the opposite side of the page.**

- **A child with autism often sees details very well but doesn't see how those details fit together, making it difficult to discern meaning in many situations.** Imagine trying to view an entire room through a telescope or a tube. Details of specific objects would be more obvious, but how the objects fit together in the room would be difficult to determine.

- **Some children may feel physical pain or possibly be blinded when lights are too bright or if there is too much visual stimulation.**

- **Eye contact can be deeply uncomfortable for a child with autism, and in fact produces great anxiety.** Research indicates that the part of the brain which causes newborns to turn toward familiar faces is activated differently for people with autism. Adults with ASD sometimes describe eye contact as so disturbing that if it's required, any other meaningful thought is challenging because it is so emotionally overwhelming.

- **A child who is not making eye contact may be listening and, indeed, paying very close attention to you.** Therefore, it is usually unwise to demand eye contact, especially when it is critical for a child to understand your words.

- **A child may be communicating that he is visually overwhelmed** when he closes his eyes, puts his head down, or intentionally stares at a wall or off into space. Suggest a baseball cap or sunglasses before going outside in bright sunlight for a child who has over-sensitive vision.

Page 4 – Taste

- **Many children with autism are very picky eaters,** sometimes having a diet consisting of less than ten foods. For some children, the sensation of hot or cold in their mouth is painful. For example, the taste of ice cream may be pleasing, but the coldness is painful. If the child is willing to force the ice cream down, he may look distressed or run around in circles.

- **Eating is related to the senses of sight, touch, and smell.** Some textures or smells may be offensive or even painful to a child, causing him to be unwilling to taste a particular food. The fear of foods is very real, and isn't easily overcome.

- **Children needing stimulation find that the sense of touch in their mouth is more sensitive than touching with their hands.** This may entice the child to put something in his mouth to try to feel it or to get some sensory stimulation from it. This may be why a child will lick or even eat unusual objects like bricks, reflectors, or sand.

- **Watch carefully to make sure a child doesn't ingest harmful things** and help minimize ridicule from his peers when it does occur. Firmly tell the child "no" and try to redirect his attention. If this is a common problem, use a consistently repeated phrase like, "Not in your mouth; this is not food." Sometimes helping a child's peers memorize a phrase to say when they see their friend putting objects in his mouth reduces ridicule because it gives peers something helpful to do.

Page 5 – Touch

- **A light touch on the arm can sometimes feel painful, like getting a shot.** Can you imagine going through each day wondering when someone might randomly give you a shot? The fear of unexpected light touch can produce much anxiety. Often, a firm touch is less painful or annoying. A gentle pat on the head or back may be distressing rather than positive.

- **Touch sensitivity may swing from high to low within the span of a few hours.** Touch seems to be the sense that swings the most quickly from over- to under-reactive.

- **Sitting in the back of a room or standing at the back of the line may be much easier** because unexpected touch is less likely. Having children line up while sitting, rather than standing, often eliminates pushing, touching, and other troublesome behaviors.

- **A child may crave deep pressure when his sense of touch is overwhelmed or during times of high anxiety.** Many children will crawl under rugs, carpets, couch cushions, blankets, or anything else that will give them a sense of even pressure. The child may be communicating that his sense of touch is out of balance. Find ways for the child to get firm, even pressure on his body.

- **Children with autism seek water, unaware of the danger it presents**. This may be because a sense of even pressure is achieved when a person is underwater.

Page 6 – Strength

- **The central nervous system is comprised of many more than five senses.** Two other senses are the vestibular sense (balance, movement, speed, and awareness of the body) and the proprioceptive sense (awareness of the position of limbs in space). Although these senses can be extremely troubling for children with autism, they are not covered in this book because it is difficult to present these concepts to young children. Learn more about these senses by reading about sensory processing disorder.

- **A child with autism may seem clumsy or have a tendency to do everything in a "heavy" way** (plopping when sitting, slamming doors, etc.) because he cannot sense how quickly he is moving, or exactly where his arm is relative to the rest of his body. People sometimes experience vestibular or proprioceptive confusion due to a medication, anesthesia, or alcohol. Imagine experiencing such confusion every day!

- **A child with autism may seem unable to be gentle with people or things, giving others the perception that he is very strong.** But in fact, children with autism generally have lower muscle tone than neurotypical children.

- **Determine the motive behind an aggressive behavior and encourage a better alternative for what a child is trying to communicate.** For example, a child may hit in order to show affection. Instead of disciplining him for hitting, teach him that a hug would be more appropriate.

- **Children with autism sometimes seem to have unending energy and want very little rest.** Allow plenty of time for exercise and teach the appropriate places and times to burn off extra energy. Certain activities, such as swinging, spinning, or jumping, are often very effective. Some children find that learning is much easier while exercising.

- **A child's boundless energy is also often coupled with a lack of fear.** This may put the child at risk of danger to himself or others. For instance, a child may suddenly run across a busy street or ride his bike down a steep hill without realizing the potential danger.

Page 7 – Pretending

- **A child with autism often does not understand abstract concepts or pretend play,** making it difficult for him to join many childhood games.

- **Rough play (wrestling, boxing, kick-boxing, etc.) can be a challenge** because the child may be unable to discriminate between a pretend punch and a real punch. Therefore, when the child does try to join in with the other children, he may hurt someone. Close supervision is needed if this kind of play is allowed at all.

- **Children with autism are literal thinkers.** Idioms (ants in your pants, butterflies in your stomach) can be confusing and scary! This thinking also leads to a strong sense of right and wrong, with very little room for shades of gray or compromise.

Page 8 – Intelligence

- **Some experts propose that the ratio of intelligence levels does not vary between people with autism and neurotypicals.** There are similar numbers of people who are extremely intelligent and people with cognitive impairments in both populations. This is very difficult to measure since there is no accurate method of IQ testing for people who have communication or social impairments or who are not willing participants in the testing.

- **Some children have amazing memories for facts or physical locations.** Having a highly developed area of specialized knowledge can cause difficulties because people see that intelligence and expect highly developed social intelligence, as well. When social intelligence is expected but turns out to be nonexistent, people often assume that the person has bad behavior rather than a lack of understanding.

- **A child does not have to be a savant in any area to have autism.** The term "savant" has been used to describe people who have unusual intellectual ability in one particular area. The most common areas are math, art, music, and memory, although a child may excel in any area. Some children with autism learn counting and the alphabet very young, some even before they can talk. However, this is not true of all children with autism.

- **Praise the child for his strengths.** Sometimes a child receives so much correction that he ends up feeling unintelligent. Search for areas to reinforce the positive and praise the child in front of his peers.

- **Working with a child in his area of strength may have a calming effect.** For example, if a child who loves the alphabet is distressed by a noisy, crowded classroom, sitting with him to write letters or singing the ABCs might help. Using a current strength or interest in order to teach a new skill can also be very helpful.

Page 9 – Playing

- **Many children with autism go through stages of being obsessed with particular toys or subjects.** The transportation industry is one of the most common obsessions. A child may line up his toys in straight lines, watch toys spin, or disassemble and reassemble toys rather than playing with them as neurotypical peers do.

- **Most children with autism want desperately to have friends and to "fit in" with their peers** but cannot make sense out of their peers' actions. Friendships can be encouraged by doing what the child with autism is doing. Sometimes, after a connection has been made this way, more meaningful interactions will occur. However, remember that meaningful social relationships do not often come quickly or easily. Sometimes persistence, coupled with several different strategies, will be required before connections are made.

Pages 11 & 12 – Talking

- **Conversations can be one-sided or seem to lack understanding.** Language is a very individualized area. As many as 40% of children with autism never talk, others begin talking very late, and still others have very sophisticated language at an early age.

- **Find ways to communicate.** Help peers understand that they are not necessarily being ignored, and encourage them to keep talking with the child.

- **Consider suggesting an appropriate answer to a peer's question if a child has the ability to talk but doesn't respond.** Anxiety may build because processing what was said and formulating an appropriate response is difficult.

- **The language of many children with autism is composed of phrases they have memorized or recently heard.** Often these phrases or scripts are from television, movies, videos, or overheard conversations. Phrases blurted out with no understandable context might be triggered by a word or sound that the child heard, or may be a way the child comforts himself. Many children will continually mumble or quote long, memorized scripts. Carefully monitoring what a child hears is important, as it can be very difficult to train a child to stop saying the memorized phrase.

Page 13 – Feelings

- **Most people with autism have difficulty reading other people's body language or facial expressions.** A person must first ascertain how another person is feeling in order to respond appropriately.

- **A child with autism may only experience emotional extremes, making maintaining emotional equilibrium difficult.** For instance, a child may feel tremendously happy or horribly sad, but may never experience moderate emotions.

- **Challenging behavior can sometimes occur because a child is feeling an emotion that is overwhelming,** or the child needs a way to communicate emotions for which he cannot find words.

- **Frequently identify a child's emotions and the emotions of other people by naming the emotion and describing how to recognize it.**

- **A normally simple task might become virtually impossible when a child is experiencing an extreme emotion.**

Page 14 – Sharing

- **Teaching sharing is difficult when a child struggles with the ability to see something from another person's perspective.** A child with autism may believe that we are all thinking the same thoughts or have only one mind. It may not occur to him that we all have unique thoughts and beliefs. A common thought process might be: *I want the toy; therefore, everyone else around also wants me to have the toy. It's ridiculous that this adult wants me to give the toy to my friend when my friend really wants me to have the toy!*

- **A child with autism may not want to share because he thrives on order and routine.** There is comfort in having the dollhouse set up "perfectly." Anyone else would mess it up if they played with it. Pretend play is very unpredictable.

- **Consider giving the child something concrete to help him understand when and with whom to share.** Statements such as "two more minutes until your turn" are often effective. Redirecting the child to another activity will sometimes help.

- **Taking turns with two people or continuing around a circle are very concrete actions, and children can do well with these skills once learned.** Teaching sharing is a long process for all children and requires patience and endurance.

Page 15 – Change

- **Children with autism feel a strong need for structure.** They need to understand what the rules are and exactly how a situation will take place. They may struggle when they expect something to happen one way, but it happens another. They may get upset if a schedule changes or something is different from normal.

- **If children with autism aren't told what to expect, they often decide for themselves what to expect.** When their prediction turns out to be incorrect, anxiety and frustration can result. When there is going to be a change to their routine, explain in advance what is going to happen next.

- **Use pictures or icons to help a child understand the order of events.** Rearrange the pictures to show a child that a change is going to take place.

- **Make smooth transitions from one activity to another.** In a classroom setting, if the children get out of control for a few moments while the teacher is switching from one activity to another, neurotypical children may be relatively easy to calm and redirect to the next activity. The child with autism will be very frustrated by this quick change. Eliminate the moments in the middle and move directly from the first activity to the second. Another option is to give specific instructions for how to behave during the transition and how to know when the transition will end.

Page 16 – Quiet Times

- **Many children with autism are capable of sitting quietly, but it may not be easy or preferred.** Find out from parents or teachers how long a child can reasonably be expected to sit quietly. Often, a hand fidget can be tremendously beneficial.

- **Determine what is reasonable, and make sure the child understands your expectations and the consequences for not sitting quietly.** Be very consistent with the enforcement of these consequences, as consistency will help the child succeed.

- **Create something concrete to demonstrate how long quiet time will last.** For instance, move an object along a line from start to finish as the quiet time continues. Other options include a strip of Velcro with a smiley face that can be moved every couple of minutes, or flipping cards with pictures of a circle that gets sequentially more filled as time progresses. Giving a concrete signal indicating when the quiet time is done may help a child wait quietly, watching for the signal.

Page 17 – Pictures

- **Use pictures or icons that can be associated with certain activities or words.** Pictures can be used to express feelings more easily than words.

- **Verbal instructions regarding choices can be overwhelming.** If a child is able to choose activities or objects, pictures may assist him in making these decisions. For example, if the child is being asked to choose between juice, water, or milk, show the child all three options and then let him choose. Icons representing various play activities can also be helpful.

- **Pictures may teach the value of communication.** When a child learns that communication helps him get what he wants, he is much more motivated to learn to communicate. This understanding usually precedes verbal language.

- **Pictures can also be used to effectively communicate consequences of actions.** Demonstrate that if this picture happens, then that picture results; or more simply, first this, then that.

Page 18-19 – Conclusion

- **In summary, a child's reaction to over-responsive or under-responsive senses can vary from complete shut-down to extreme emotional outbursts.** The child's response is often driven by the natural "fight or flight" response. We should be constantly studying and evaluating situations in order to try to understand what a child is trying to communicate through his behavior.

- **The goal is to train a child to behave appropriately, not excuse inappropriate behavior because we understand the challenges.** However, understanding the possible causes for behavior is the first step toward positive change.

- **Children with ASD desire to have friends, but often find it difficult to understand and relate to their peers.** It is likely that children can be helped to establish meaningful relationships with peers when a person is patient, consistent, and observant. Remember that a meaningful relationship for a person with ASD may not look "typical," but it can still be very meaningful and also very rewarding!

18 Signs and Symptoms of an Autism Spectrum Disorder

- Delayed, little, or no speech OR sophisticated, adult-like speech
- Speech patterns that frequently echo other people's exact words
- Reversed pronouns ("You want a cookie please"—meaning "I want a cookie")
- Seeming to talk *at* people rather than talking *with* them
- Absence of nonverbal communication, such as pointing, gesturing, or leading someone by the hand
- Sometimes seems not to hear or understand simple directions
- Hands cover ears at unexpected sounds (indicating pain or fear)
- Lack of eye contact or difficulty making eye contact with others (appears to be looking "through" you)
- Walking on tiptoes consistently when shoes are removed
- Hyperactivity, requiring very little sleep, or extreme lack of activity
- Difficulty playing with peers (doesn't join in or seem to understand the pretend play of others)
- Unusual methods of playing with toys for long periods of time (repeatedly lining things up or twirling them)
- Seems unaware of the feelings of others (no reaction to someone getting hurt or someone crying)
- Little desire to share happy moments with someone else, not looking to see if someone else is looking at the same thing
- Strong need for sameness, routine, or repetition (not wanting to take a different route to the store)
- Doesn't seem to learn from typical consequences
- An apparent lack of fear
- Unusual pain responses (over-response or lack of response)

10 Quick Strategies for Helping a Child with Autism

1. **Simplify your language,** especially when the child is frustrated. Say, "Come here, please," instead of saying, "Mommy wants you to come here and stay close to me so you will be safe when we are walking in the parking lot." Hand gestures may also be helpful.

2. **Give the child ways to cope with sensory problems.** For example, use earplugs or headphones if the child is over-stimulated by sound. Balance stimulating social activities with quiet, non-social times. People with autism spectrum disorders "fill up quickly" on social events. Determine the calming sensory experiences (deep pressure, squeeze hugs, lights off) and incorporate them into daily activities, helping calm a child's heightened nervous system.

3. **If the child can read, use written words to communicate during stressful situations.** Verbal instructions may be more difficult to process and less concrete. In order to manage a stressful situation, we must choose what stimuli we can pay attention to and what we must ignore. Help by eliminating as many stimuli as possible.

4. **Give the child a visual and an oral schedule.** Use pictures, written words, or objects to communicate what is coming next. Crossing something off a list or removing an icon representing each activity when it is finished provides comfort and security to the child. Perhaps the biggest advantage of using a visual schedule is that it offers an effective way to communicate that a change is going to happen before it actually does, thus eliminating some challenging moments.

5. **Use a calendar to show special events, trips, or vacations.** Use pictures or written words to make those events clear. The child can cross off each day of the week to get a visual picture of how close the special event is getting.

6. **Use the "First/Then" strategy.** Using pictures or words, communicate to the child, "First brush your teeth, then watch a video. First teeth, then video."

7. **Use the phrase, "The rule is_____,"** especially for social rules. Be sure to tell the child the reason for that rule.

8. **Purposefully catch the child doing the right thing** and then praise his action specifically. It is usually very effective to include comments such as, "What a smart thing to do!" Children often pride themselves on intelligence.

9. **Be consistent.** The more calm and consistent you can be, the safer the child will feel. Kids like to know that "whenever I do this, that happens." This doesn't mean that you need to be harsh, just stick to the rules and expectations that you have established.

10. **Give the child choices.** Provide pictures or written choices for the child (chicken or cheeseburger? Play outside or Play-Doh?). If the child has trouble making choices, help him pick one of two choices and follow through with it. After some guided practice, he will likely make an independent choice.

Recommended Reading

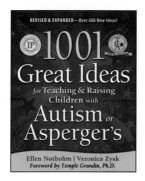

1001 Great Ideas for Teaching and Raising Children with Autism or Asperger's
(Ellen Notbohm and Veronica Zysk, 2010)

ASD to Z: Basic Information, Support, and Hope
(Laurel A. Falvo, 2008)

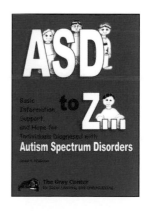

Asperger's in Pink
(Julie Clark, 2010)

Autism … What Does It Mean To Me?
(Catherine Faherty, 2014)

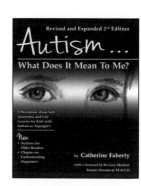

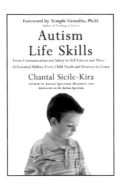

Autism Life Skills: From Communication and Safety to Self-Esteem and More
(Chantal Sicile-Kira, 2008)

Behavior Solutions for the Inclusive Classroom
(Beth Aune, Beth Burt, and Peter Gennaro, 2010)

The Complete Guide to Asperger's Syndrome
(Tony Attwood, 2008)

Different Like Me: My Book of Autism Heroes
(Jennifer Elder, 2005)

My Book Full of Feelings: How to Control and React to the Size of Your Emotions
(Amy Jaffe and Luci Gardner, 2006)

The New Social Story Book, Revised and Expanded 15th Anniversary Edition
(Carol Gray, 2015)

No More Meltdowns: Positive Strategies for Managing and Preventing Out-of-Control Behavior
(Jed Baker, 2008)

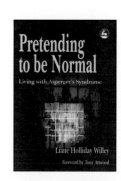

Pretending to Be Normal: Living with Asperger's Syndrome
(Liane Holliday Willey, 1999)

Sensitive Sam
(Marla Roth-Fisch, 2010)

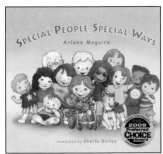

Special People, Special Ways
(Arlene Maguire, 2000)

Thinking in Pictures
(Temple Grandin, 2010)

Friends Learn About Tobin
(Diane Murrell, 2001)

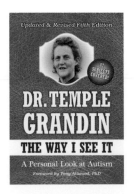

The Way I See It, 5th edition
(Temple Grandin, 2020)

About the Author and Illustrator

Beverly Bishop was determined to help her son with autism fit in with his peers by fostering understanding and tolerance among her son's friends and schoolmates. She wrote *My Friend with Autism* for her son's elementary teachers and peers. Beverly conducts autism awareness trainings for law enforcement officers and teaches safety and educational classes around the country for parents, family members, professionals, college students, and other community members. Beverly has also taught in both public and private schools and has enjoyed managing a non-profit organization. Beverly and her husband, Thad, are very proud of their now-adult son with autism, Sebastian, who has brought them immense joy as he has overcome many obstacles in life with great resilience and brilliant humor, proving that autism can indeed be a blessing to many.

Craig Bishop, Sebastian's uncle, worked as an art educator in Michigan Public Schools for thirty years. He retired from Western Michigan University in Kalamazoo as an instructor in Art Education, where he also received his early training in art. Craig enjoys painting, illustrating, teaching art classes, and being a grandparent to Henry and Lucy.